It's About Time, Max!

by Kitty Richards
Illustrated by Gioia Fiammenghi

The Kane Press
New York

Book Design/Art Direction: Roberta Pressel

Library of Congress Cataloging-in-Publication Data

Richards, Kitty.
    It's about time, Max!/by Kitty Richards; illustrated by Gioia Fiammenghi.
      p. cm. — (Math matters)
    Summary: When Max misplaces his digital watch, he replaces it with an analog watch that he does not know how to read and finds himself late for everything.
    ISBN 1-57565-088-6 (pbk. : alk. paper)
    [1. Clocks and watches—Fiction. 2. Time—Fiction. 3. Tardiness—Fiction.]
I. Fiammenghi, Gioia, ill. II. Title. III. Series.
PZ7.R3875It 2000
[Fic]—DC21

98-51118
CIP
AC

10 9 8 7 6 5 4 3 2 1

First published in the United States of America in 2000 by The Kane Press.
Printed in Hong Kong.

Time to wake up, Max!" called my mom.

I yawned and checked my watch. Seven o'clock. I wake up at the same time every morning. Then I can do all the things I need to do before I catch the school bus at 8:05. I'm never late.

Every morning
from 7:05 to 7:15
I take a shower.

From 7:15 to 7:20
I brush my teeth.

From 7:20 to 7:30
I get dressed.

From 7:30 to 7:45
I eat my Crispy
Critters. Yum!

From 7:45 to 7:55
I walk my dog, Zombie.
(I call him that 'cause I
love monster movies!)

Then I go and wait for the
bus. It comes at 8:05. Mrs. Dunn,
the driver, is on time every day,
just like me.

All right, all right. I have to
admit that for a while I was
really late. Here's how it started.

"Time to wake up, Max," my mom called.

I showered and brushed my teeth. I got
dressed. Then I reached for my digital watch.

It wasn't on my night stand. Or in my
bathrobe pocket, or on the sink! Oh no!

I tied my Air Turbo Gravity-Defying sneakers
and ran downstairs.

"Hey," I said. "Has anybody seen my watch?"
"Nope," said Mom and Dad.
"Nope," said my sister, Ann.
"What am I going to do?" I moaned.
"I have a watch you can borrow," said Ann.

"You'd better hurry up," said Mom. "It's already 7:50."

Uh-oh. I was five minutes behind schedule! I shoved the watch in my pocket, called Zombie, and zoomed out the door.

When we got to the corner, I decided
to check the time.

Yikes! It wasn't a digital watch. This one
had hands on it!

What time was it? I couldn't tell. I ran
home as fast as I could.

Oops. My mom was waiting outside
with a not-very-happy look on her face.
"You just missed the bus!" she said.

So Mom had to drive me to school and write a late note. I was sooooo embarrassed.

The next day was Saturday. I was all excited because I was going to my first surprise party ever. Dad was going to drive me.

He kept yawning. "In case I nod off, be sure to wake me at 5:30," he said. "We should leave then."

I stared at Dad. My parents are sort of old-fashioned. There wasn't a single digital clock in the house.

"Five-thirty?" I said, stalling.

"You know," said Dad, "when the big hand is on the 6 and the little hand is between the 5 and the 6?" He smiled.

That made it a little easier. "Okay," I said.

When the little hand was by the 6, and the big hand was on the 5, I woke up my dad. He wasn't very happy. Not at all.

"Max!" he said, "I asked you to wake me at 5:30. It's 6:25!"

I must have mixed up the hands. We drove straight to the party, but I missed the best part—when everyone jumps out and yells "SURPRISE!" What a bummer.

That Sunday Mom and I went to the movies to see "The Boy Who Ate Cleveland." Like I said, I love monster movies. So does Mom.

We got to the mall early.

"I want to go to Jay's," I said. "He might have some new monster comics for me."

"And I want to go to the CD store," said Mom. "I'll meet you here at a quarter after three."

"Um...maybe I'll go with you," I said. Then I remembered that the comic book store had a big digital clock on the wall.

"Okay," I said, "a quarter after three is fine."

17

I looked at comic books for a while.
Then, when the clock said a quarter after
three, I went to meet my mom.

"Max, I've been waiting for ten minutes," Mom said. "The movie already started!"

"But I'm on time," I said. "It's a quarter after. A quarter is 25 cents, and it's 3:25."

"No, Max," Mom said. "Time doesn't work like money. A quarter after three is 3:15, not 3:25."

So we missed the movie. I felt pretty bad.

That night Mom called me into the living room. The whole family was there. So were papers with clocks and numbers.

"Max," said Mom, "we couldn't help noticing that you can't tell time."

I felt myself turning red. "But I *can* tell time—on my digital watch," I said. "Besides, I have a headache."

"Relax," Dad said. "We've made up a little game to help you out."

"Like a treasure hunt," Mom added.

"With a prize at the end," Ann said.

"Yeah?" I said. This almost sounded like fun!

Dad said that I'd need a few hints about telling time. We talked about some stuff I think I had in school.

Ann drew pictures for me.

Then Mom told me this rhyme.

The little hand has all the power.
That is why it tells the hour.

That was easy to remember. "Okay," I said. "Where's my first clue?"

minute hand

5 minutes
5 minutes
5 minutes
5 minutes

hour
hand

You count by fives
To find the minutes
An hour is 60 minutes
A half hour is 30 minutes
A quarter hour
is 15 minutes.

The long hand
shows the minutes
The short hand
shows the hour

Mom handed me a card. I started to read it.
"I'll give you a hint—" said Ann.
"No," I said. "I can do it!"

I thought to myself. The hour hand was on 7, so that meant it was 7–something. And since the minute hand was on 12, it was 7 o'clock! This wasn't so hard!

So what do I do at 7 o'clock every morning? I wake up! The next clue must be in my room!

To find the first clue
read this little rhyme,
Where are you each morning
at this time?

But where in my room? Ah-hah! At 7:00, I was in bed! I picked up my pillow and there was the next clue.

Hickory dickory dock! What time is on this clock?

Okay. The little hand was on 7 and the big hand was on 1. I remembered how you count by fives to find the minutes. So, since the big hand was on 1, that meant it was five minutes after 7. What do I do at 7:05?

I take a shower! I ran to the bathroom.
And there on the soap dish was another
clue. It was a little soggy, but I could read it.

Hmmm. The little hand was on 7 and
the big hand was on 3. So it was fifteen
minutes after 7. I brush my teeth at 7:15.

Sure enough, the next clue was wrapped around my toothbrush!

The little hand was between 7 and 8. The big hand was on 6. So it was thirty minutes after 7. At 7:30 each day I eat my breakfast. This was getting easier and easier!

Right again!
My clue was on the kitchen table.

This clock clue is
not so Tough.
Just think—
Who says ruff ruff ruff!

"Zombie!" I yelled. "I walk Zombie at 7:45!"
Zombie came running into the kitchen.
Mom, Dad, and Ann were close behind.
"Congratulations!" they shouted.

Then I saw an envelope in Zombie's mouth.
Inside were tickets to the Monster Movie
Marathon! I couldn't believe it! I never
thought I'd get to go. "All right!" I said.

I never did find my digital watch—but
that doesn't matter. Now I can tell time
on all kinds of clocks.

And, as I said, I'm never late. Sometimes, I'm even early!

Time Chart

There are 60 minutes in 1 hour.

4:00

You can write: 4:00

There are 30 minutes in a half hour.

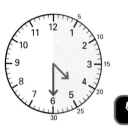

4:30

You can write: 4:30

There are 15 minutes in a quarter hour.

4:1

You can write: 4:15

Here are some ways to say the time.

2:00

two o'clock

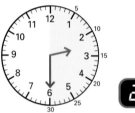

2:30

30 minutes after 2, or
two thirty, or half past 2

2:15

15 minutes after 2, or
two fifteen, or
a quarter after 2

2:45

45 minutes after 2, or
two forty-five, or
a quarter to 3

2:20

20 minutes after 2, or
two twenty

2:55

55 minutes after 2, or
two fifty-five